NEVER FEAR,
FLIP THE DIP IS HERE

by Philip Hanft · pictures by Thomas B. Allen

Dial Books for Young Readers New York

Published by Dial Books for Young Readers
A Division of Penguin Books USA Inc.
375 Hudson Street
New York, New York 10014

Printed in Hong Kong by South China Printing Company (1988) Limited

First Edition
W
1 3 5 7 9 10 8 6 4 2

The full-color artwork was prepared with charcoal, pastel,
and colored pencils. It was then scanner-separated and reproduced
in red, blue, yellow, and black halftones.

Library of Congress Cataloging in Publication Data
Hanft, Philip. Never fear, Flip the Dip is here / by Philip Hanft;
pictures by Thomas B. Allen.
p. cm.
Summary: Flip, upset about not being able to play baseball very
well, acquires self-confidence and sports skills from Buster, a
former minor league ballplayer.
ISBN 0-8037-0897-1.— ISBN 0-8037-0899-8 (lib. bdg.)
[1. Baseball—Fiction. 2. Self-confidence—Fiction.]
I. Allen, Thomas B. (Thomas Burt), 1928– ill. II. Title.
PZ7. H1943Ne   1991   [E]—dc20 90-3385 CIP AC

For my son Max
P. H.

To my first good teacher,
John F. Richardson
T. A.

Flip wanted to play baseball. But none of the kids wanted to play baseball with Flip. Flip couldn't catch. Flip couldn't throw. And Flip was two years younger than the kids who played baseball at the playground.

One day after Fat Ralph chased Flip under the bleachers, Flip walked home through the alleys so no one could see him crying. He tried to keep his chin up like his dad always told him to. But every time he thought about some of the names the kids called him, his chin started to quiver and more tears came.

Flip looked at the old baseball mitt his dad had given him. It had belonged to his dad when he was a kid. No wonder the kids laughed at him. No one played with gloves like that anymore. Flip threw the glove in a trash can behind an old garage.

"You don't really want to toss that glove, do you?" a voice boomed from out of nowhere.

Flip looked around, feeling a little ashamed. A man, wiping an artist's brush with a paint-stained rag, stepped through a darkened doorway in the back of the garage.

"What's your name, kid?"

"Flip."

The man picked Flip's glove out of the trash and slapped it against his leg to knock off the dust.

"Hey, man, this is the same kind of glove I use. Why do you want to throw away a prime mitt like this?"

"It's old and stupid. And besides, the kids won't let me play anyway. They all laugh at me and call me Flip the Dip."

"I know how you feel, Flip. My name is Buster." The man examined the glove affectionately. "Ooooh, this is fine. Where'd you get this glove, Flip?"

"It was my dad's when he was a kid."

The man slipped his left hand into the glove, made smooth and soft and oily with age. He drove his large fist into the pocket with a loud smack. He reached down for an imaginary grounder, scooping it off the ground from between his legs. He jumped high for a fly ball against a centerfield wall some-where in the sunlight of his past.

"Let's see the ball, kid."

The man drilled the ball into the webbing of the mitt. Once, twice. *Thwack. Thwack.* How he loved that sound, the man said. Then he gave the ball a light toss in the air and popped it off the inside of his right elbow as it came down, catching it easily in his bare hand.

Leaning over, his face close to Flip's, the man spoke gently.

"Kid, it's not the glove's fault you can't throw or catch. Ask your dad, I'll bet he'll teach you how to use it."

Flip's blue eyes brightened, then quickly clouded over.

"My dad's in the Navy. On sea duty."

"Okay, Flip the Dip, I'll teach you." Buster handed the glove back. "You can usually find me upstairs in my studio. We got a deal?"

So Flip found a friend. Almost every day Flip and Buster practiced. Flip told
Buster about Fat Ralph. So they drew a picture of Ralph on Buster's garage
door. They drew a strike zone next to him and Flip learned to work his pitches.
High and inside. Low and inside. Hard down the middle.

Buster talked about playing in the minor leagues. Traveling by bus, staying in
dirty motels, eating bad meals. But never, ever wanting to give it up. Because
more than anything, Buster loved the feeling of green grass singing beneath
his feet and the whistle-white ball sailing across the summer sky into his glove.

Buster taught Flip about keeping your eye on the ball. About keeping focused on what you're doing. Where the ball is. Where you want it to go. Where the other players are, what they're doing.

And so it went for most of Flip's summer. Flip and Buster talked and practiced. Flip threw the ball. Flip caught the ball. Flip pitched the ball. Flip caught the ball. Flip pegged the ball. Flip caught the ball. Fly balls. Ground balls. Line drives. Over and over and over. And after every dropped ball, every flubbed grounder, every wild pitch, Buster's magic words of encouragement would leap through the air ahead of the next throw.

"No problem, Flip. You got it. No problem."

Sometimes Flip would stay and have dinner in Buster's studio above the garage. Buster would cook giant, juicy, square hamburgers, which he called slab burgers. Flip thought Buster should start a hamburger chain called Buster Burgers. Buster said he'd have to sell a lot more paintings first.

Flip liked to look at Buster's paintings and sculptures around the apartment. Most of them he didn't understand. But they made him feel good.

Buster said he began drawing when he was Flip's age. Next to baseball it was the only thing he had ever wanted to do. He said painting and playing baseball were a lot alike. That baseball was art too.

By Flip's mother's standards, Buster's apartment was a mess. But Flip loved it. All over the walls, where there wasn't a painting or sculpture, Buster had taped pictures and headlines torn out of magazines and books. He said they were his idea starters. Laughing, he called his studio the world's largest filing cabinet.

One steamy, late-August afternoon Flip, dreaming about fly balls and line drives, forgot to avoid the playground. He didn't notice the third- and fourth-graders picking sides.

"Hey, Dipster. Ya wanna play?" Fat Ralph yelled across the shabby baseball diamond.

"Me?" Flip yelled back, ready to ditch at the slightest sign of treachery.

"Yeah, you, pipsqueak. Right field."

Flip unhooked his glove from his belt loop and trotted across the infield, past Fat Ralph.

"Keep your eyes open, your mouth closed, and don't drop nothin'...including your pants," Ralph sniggered. The rest of the kids laughed.

Flip found his position in right field. He made a fist and smacked the pocket of his glove. I'm going to show these guys, he thought. Just wait until someone hits one to me. Straight to the relay. Like a rocket. I'll burn it....

"Hey, Dip. Wake up." The ball rolled past Flip.

Flip grabbed the ball and pegged it to Fat Ralph. Ralph reached up with his glove. The ball connected with a loud *thwack*. Fat Ralph looked at the ball in his glove. And then up at Flip and back again at the ball.

"Okay, Dipster. One more chance."

Flip stopped dreaming and started playing. His eyes never left the ball. *Whack.* Frankie Williams hit a high fly ball over Jenny Turner at first base. Flip grabbed it out of the air and *thwack*, drove it into Fat Ralph's glove.

Flip was hot. He picked them out of the air. Off the grass. Out of the dirt. Ralph and his pals couldn't believe this kid with the dorky glove.

Ralph was hot too. He'd just struck out the last six batters. But now he had to face the mega-boy, mini-man Stanley Manley, a switch-hitting MVP from the 24th Street Little League.

Fat Ralph went through his windup and released the ball. Stanley could see it clearly. The stitches spinning. The way it rose and then dropped to the outside. Stanley put his entire body into the swing.

The ball was a rocket. It was a bullet. It was a knockout punch in Madison Square Garden. It was a bull's-eye, right between Fat Ralph's beady little eyes.

Ralph hit the ground.

No one moved. No one spoke.

Finally, after a few moments, which seemed like a few years to everyone except Fat Ralph, the flattened pitcher picked himself up. Staggering he dusted himself off, grabbed his glove and, without a word, weaved off the diamond toward home.

The only sound came from the flies buzzing in and out of the open mouths of the eight ballplayers left on the field.

Not until Fat Ralph had rounded the corner a block away did Flip and his teammates turn their attention to Tardy Charlie Klinker leaning on his bat in the batter's box. Tardy Charlie was always late for school, and everyone knew it was because his dad made him do two hundred push-ups every morning. No one messed with Tardy Charlie. Not even Fat Ralph.

Freddie Solomon jogged to home plate to huddle with the catcher.

"Who's gonna pitch?" Freddie Solomon whimpered.

The catcher looked at Tardy Charlie and swallowed hard. Tardy Charlie, showing a mouthful of yellow, mossy teeth, grinned back.

A shudder went through the entire field of players, then in one smooth motion, all heads turned toward the little kid standing in right field.

"Hey, Dipster. You pitch!" Freddie yelled.

Flip, unafraid, stared back in silent defiance. He knew he could pitch.

"Okay," Freddie pleaded. *"Paleeeeze."*

Flip trotted toward the pitcher's mound. I'm not afraid of Tardy Charlie, he thought. I can get him out.

Flip the Dip checked first base. Then second. He kicked the dust at his feet. He inspected the stitching on his dad's old glove. He rolled the hard leather ball on the tips of his five right digits. It felt cool, light, and familiar. He shrugged the tension out of his shoulders. He squinted at Tardy Charlie. Finally, in one smooth, liquid motion, Flip launched the perfect, white orb off his calloused fingertips.

The ball sailed. It danced. It snapped. It jumped.

Tardy Charlie's bat split the air with a sharp crack, catapulting the pale ball toward the sun. An hour, a day, a year passed as Flip watched the ball rise and fall against the sky. He stepped forward, then back, at last reaching up with his funny old mitt and snatching the ball out of the air.

Flip the Dip looked at the ball in his mitt and let out a deep sigh.

Jenny Turner threw her glove in the air and ran in circles like a crazed dog. Freddie Solomon yelped like a wild coyote. The third-base kid whooped and danced. The entire infield quickly became lost in a cloud of dust and wild cheering.

Through the rising dust Flip spotted Buster in the bleachers. The big man smiled and raised an old baseball glove high in a gesture of triumph.

Grinning, Flip gave the ball a light toss in the air and popped it off the inside of his right elbow as it came down, catching it easily in his bare hand.

"Never fear, Flip the Dip is here," he whispered.